C000155929

*God was my
leader from birth*

God was my leader from birth

MIRACLE OF GOD

JEANIE BREEDWELL

Copyright © Jeanie Breedwell.

All rights reserved. No part of this book may be reproduced in any form or by any electronic or mechanical means, including information storage and retrieval systems, without permission in writing from the publisher, except by reviewers, who may quote brief passages in a review.

ISBN: 978-1-64826-992-9   (Paperback Edition)
ISBN: 978-1-64826-993-6   (Hardcover Edition)
ISBN: 978-1-64826-991-2   (E-book Edition)

Some characters and events in this book are fictitious. Any similarity to real persons, living or dead, is coincidental and not intended by the author.

Book Ordering Information

Phone Number: 347-901-4929 or 347-901-4920
Email: info@globalsummithouse.com
Global Summit House
www.globalsummithouse.com

Printed in the United States of America

When I was a little Girl, in Alabama in north of the state, my mother told my brother and me about Jesus. She told us many stories and we were just sitting around the fireplace. That is what we do. Look at the fire burning in the old fireplace.

Mama told us about the one who died for us.

Mama was like an open book. She would open her mouth out and it would come sometimes that she would talk for a long time.

She had so much to feed us her kids with the word of God;

And since that was the only thing we knew, it was a Tradition in our home. My mama loves us, her kids.

She carried us to the old country Church. We had to walk to church, no car.

A friend of Mama told me she carried me when I was first born.

We all sing in the church. Mama brought singing home with her. I can hear singing in the kitchen like a bird when we all get to heaven.

Won't it be wonderful there; many more songs; I listen to her sing most of the time.

You could find me in the yard playing.

That is the memories I cannot forget. Mama praying. Mama would pray, she got an answer.

She would be on her knees for hours and read her Bible every day.

Back to the time Mama was talking about this family.

They had so many kids. It was church night then mama and daddy had to leave. Some of the kids we're left at home.

While they're gone, someone knock at the door. The kids ran to the door. It was a man. They welcome him in the picture caught his eyes.

He was telling the kids about Jesus then he left. The kids look outside and he was gone.

When the family got home, mother was so happy, she shouted.

She knew it was an angel sent by God to protect her children.

Mama did not tell us about her childhood.

My grandfather pass away before I was born. My grandmother lost some of her children.

My mama had to play with her brothers like me.

Grandma keep things hidden inside of her.

Just a few things she told me like her maiden name. I know we were poor people.

We lived in grandma's old house. No electric. It was never painted. The water was from a well. No bathroom inside. If we did not get our water from the well before night, we had to carry flash light.

I was afraid to go outside after dark.

Sometimes, God had that old moon bright for us to see where we were going.

We went to bed early. Got up with when we heard the rooster crew.

We had no television or anything to keep us awake.

Mama made sure we say our prayers at night time.

The next morning, it was School time. Could not be late.

The School bus would not wait for us.

One day, I saw the bus at the top of the hill. I cried because I knew it was my fault and Mama would not like it.

She would see me coming home dragging in like an old hound dog.

I would try to make up for it and go into the kitchen. Get a stool. Wash the dishes in that old dishpan.

Instead of giving me what I deserved, mama had me.

She knew the house would be clean.

I had a very good Mama. I thank God every day for giving me her.

I missed her so much.

I think about the title of my Book.

With God, Without God.

When I'm at home, I do what mama wanted me to do.

God was number one in Mama's life. She love him so much.

The one thing my brother and me like was Christmas.

We did not get much but what we did get is what we liked.

We liked the snow. We watched it fall on the ground from the window.

Everything would be covered.

I did not liked the cold weather, but, you take the bad with the good.

I did not have a sister to grow up with.

She got married while I was a little girl. Her name was Rose.

She was older than me. France was younger than me.

God took her when she was very young. My sister Rose, later I will see them one day. I am sure in heaven.

After France got killed in Chicago, her and her friend Barbra walking across the street. A big truck hit them.

I went to stay with daddy in the windy state.

Maxine put me in School.

I met a girl Name Carol.

I was staying the night with Carol when a man broke into our house. He told Maxine daddy wanted money.

She told him my dad was at work. It was a lie.

We do not know what would happen.

After that my brother sled on the reel in the hall. This man was scared he left.

Daddy went to court nothing happen.

Carol and I went to the drug store many times.

We played together. We live on the same street.

My little sister got run over in front of our window.

I live there around too years.

One day after work, daddy come in said, "lets pack we are leaving going to Alabama".

He took me to grandma's house, his Mama I did not like.

I wanted to live with my mama and grandma. I missed my family.

One day I ran away going to see mama and grandma.

Johnson and I hid and they did not find me.

After they left, grandma said I had to go back. I did.

Later on Grandma passed away.

I rode the bus by the church. Got off to be at Grandma's funeral.

I think Grandma got mad. Later on she took me to mama.

I was so happy to see my family.

I felt so bad losing my Grandma. She was my world.

She made me some dresses when my Birthday come around.

She gave me money to buy what I wanted.

She loved the lord so much.

One day I will see her. I know.

Now I want to go further into my future.

I did not have any nice clothes.

I did not have shoes for my feet. I was made fun at School.

Before Grandma passed, I would come home crying and she would hold me telling me they were jealous of me because I was so pretty.

She had words that made me feel better. After that everything was ok.

When grandma passed, I felt like I was all by myself.

So along she would take the pain away.

So one day I quit School.

The cops pick me up. They put me in jail for not going to School.

I stayed there for a while until they had room for me at the training School for girls.

I was so scared. Lots of girls they put me in a room and lock it at night.

It was nice there. I learn some things like cooking, clean our room, and wash our clothes.

We got to go outside after we were there for a while.

Saturday night after move we had a candy bar and at Christmas we got lots of things from different people.

I went to School. Made my first dress. We had skating ring. We had fun there.

We pass the television around.

There were three cottages at the training School. We made everything from scratch.

My mama came one time to take me off for the weekend.

I really like that the weekend went by so fast. She bought me things to take back to the School.

I did go to church with a lady. She come to the School and pick me up. She was really nice.

I did miss my mama.

She wrote me letters. I was glad to receive them. She told me I would get out soon. She had faith in God.

I would tell her no Mama, I was there for a while.

I got mail from a preacher

Mother gave him my address.

I was like any other kid growing up did not believe mother. I wanted to.

I know God took care of us kids.

I was there for almost seventeen months.

When I came up for parole I was scared that I will not be coming home. They asked me questions about what I learned. I told them the best I could. I did have few surprises on my journey.

When I left there they forgot to tell me that I was not going to my mother's. They're taking me to a foster home.

I stayed there for some time. They were nice people and had good meals to eat.

I got to pick cotton with them.

They had two little kids. They were so cute. They finally got word.

My mother was in Florida with my two brothers.

The people I stay with did not want me to go.

I was ready to go into my future. The worker put me on the gray hound headed south. I did not know what was in store for my future. It did not look too bright because I had no address. No way but the dear lord to get me to Florida.

I sat on the bus just looking around to see if anyone was looking at me. I was seventeen years old. I never been to Florida before. I guess I will be ok.

My mother and brothers were there.

It had been so long since I had seen them. I got to the Bus stop. I did not know where I was.

The two ladies help me see if I had my mother's address in my case. I did not have one.

God was smiling down on me that day because as I step outside, I saw my brother coming down the sidewalk. He know it was me.

He told me I was early. They were looking for me. Later I was happy to be there.

It was a little ways to where mother was. She was waiting on me to get there even though she know I would be later on coming to her doorsteps. I can see her waiting for me walking through the house saying where is my Baby girl at. I know she prayed for me because when she saw me coming, she run to meet me.

So happy to see me it had been so long.

You could see the smile on my face. My little brother was happy too. We had so much to talk about my future.

My mother and my brothers went to church on 441 that has been lots of years.

It is where they have funeral now.

Have seen so many of my own family there to say bye to them. Telling them that I will see them again in heaven.

My mother had many friends that went to the same Church. One of them had a daughter name Brenda. She became my close friend.

We did things together. That is how I met the father of my loving children.

We were married for eight years.

We just could not get along even though we did have time to go to Church.

Before we got married we had a good time.

I give God, mother, and my brother Raymond credit, my mother.

When I brought anyone to our house she talk to them about the lord.'

I never understand what mother was saying. I hate to say this but it embarrassed me at that time but mother did not care, she would preached to me. I am happy she did.

Mother loved the lord. She let everyone know it. That is how I feel now.

It hurts me to know there are so many people that do not love Jesus. They think they have more time than the preacher told them.

I know different. I pray for sinners. I hope God lead them the right way.

Get their house in order before the rapture.

We do not have much longer Jesus did not promised us anytime.

It puts tears in my eyes when I know so many people going to hell.

I thank God every day for the ones who pray for me.

My mother and grandma are on the top list of thanks.

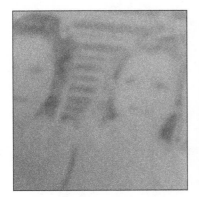

When my mother passed away, later on in my life I wonder who will pray for me since mother is gone.

That is when my world stop turning.

I change my life. The devil had me in his web. I did not care anymore. I lost my mother. Had nightmares many years.

After she was gone I started drinking, smoking, and did things that was wrong.

If Jesus had come been left behind, sad to say.

Thank God for watching over me. Keeping me safe when I did not care I was wrong.

God love me just the same. I was really deep in sin. Lost all the morals of my life.

Did not think what mother taught me. I did not care.

Did not want the memories come back. I had buried them in my

Soul.

All along with what mother had taught me, telling me what to do, I was going in the wrong direction.

To lose the good things

I was always to remember

It was not anything for me to go to asleep.

Forget the day.

I miss my mother so much.

I was all along my husband. I was married to for eight years. Left me and the kids.

I do not blame him for everything. I had my self to blame as well.

Marrying so young, mother tried to tell me not jump into the frying pan into the fire. I did not listen.

I just wanted someone to love me. No one could break that chain bound to me except Jesus.

I was running from him. It was so much different since mother was gone. I just stay in that hole of sin. I had buried myself in it and swallowed me whole.

Sinking so low I did not try to get out.

I lost my confidence tried to lose anyone that wanted to get near me because of my little girls.

I did not want anyone in my life for good.

Did not trust them. I had heard of stepdad bother other children not mind. I would not let that happen.

If I was left along the rest of my life, it did not pass my mind. I love my kids.

The devil don't care if you want to go to Church as long as you keep doing his work.

I was not thinking 'about my self is part of without God.

I did things I was not proud of. I could not start over, could not go back.

I did try to be a person that wants to go to Church, living the best I could.

I met Jerry, my next husband.

A friend told me about him.

His wife left him and to small children for another man. We married in 1974. I don't think we belong together. His children would not let him forget their mother and no one could blame them. They wanted their mother and dad together.

It did not change anything. He left me for another women then I went on with my life.

In 1984, I started up another love.

Lived with a man from Georgia. His name is Bud. He just come out of the army from 68 to 72. I met him in 1973.

He wanted to stay with his dad. His mom passed away in 1973.

We went to Georgia he stayed.

We got married. We were married for 22 years.

I was going thought so much with him. He was drunk most of our time together. I never saw him come home without him all booze up.

I cried so many times and prayed for him to change.

We were separated most of our marriage. He was under doctor care before he passed away.

I stayed with my daughter's lots until 2004. His sister called and asked if I would come take care of him. He was coming out of the hospital. He looked like a frog. Swelled up, his liver was bad. I jump right in. Started taking care of him.

With God's help, I had to wait on him like a Baby. Wash his clothes, bed clothes, cook his meals three times a day with snacks between the nurses from hospice came with him.

I tried to take care of him the best I could. He still was going to the hospital most of the time.

I went to the hospital I could not believe he was going to die because one trip to the hospital I told him, if he dies, he would not make it to heaven.

I want to go back when I went out. I did not feel good about myself.

I made it home. Olen wanted to tell me about myself.

I need to change my life. He said God told him to tell me.

I felt the spirit of God. I knew it was true what he was saying.

Sorry to admit it but I had been playing around with God. Now I had to stop and mean business with him.

I cannot hold on to the enemy and God at the same time. Tt will not work so, I told Bud, he said if I change he would leave me. I told him he had to leave.

While we were at his sisters, we both prayed every night. He was so proud of me changing, telling everyone I had change, getting back where I left off.

We moved in with my daughter Alice.

We were there for a while. He got worse. We put him in a VA hospital.

He was there a little bit.

He went to a nursing home. That is where it all began. He pull his feeding tube out of his stomach. He was sent back to the hospital. That was 2006 he passed away.

September the 10th, one month later, Alice my daughter passed away.

So my world stood still. I put my trust in Jesus. He has pulled US through it all.

I could not go one day without him. I moved on with my life.

Sister Ruth told me about my next husband Ricky Dobbs. We were together in Apopka. I told him about my friends Sue and Jerry Farmer on our way to Wildwood. We all got along okay. We went to Church together, did some things we like to do.

He asked me to marry him, I said yes. He bought my rings. We set the date for May 16. We had started back to Apopka.

Sue called me about a house. We looked at it and liked it.

Our first house. We got married and all our plans were carried out by Sister Ruth.

Was so good to help us. We have been married for 9 years now

I do not want to stop here. We live there for some time. We got us two dogs. I name my dog Patty and Ricky dog lit.

Ricky we all went to Alabama. We move in with my Sister, daughter and stay for a while. The storms made me change my mind.

We came back to Florida in 2012. God was with us again. We move into a motel. Our friends again found us a place to live.

We have been in one room for 8 years. Before the air condition went out we lost our two dogs in 2017. I miss them so much.

\

Little Ricky went missing. He has been gone for some time. I feel like he is with Patty in heaven.

One day I will see them again. Later on, we pray to the lord to give us Buddy and another Patty.

She won't take the other ones place but she is my Baby.

When I brought her home, I took a change. Put her leash on her she, broke loose and ran away, scared me. I prayed, please lord do not let anything happen to her. Jesus was with me, he had the devil people to help me find her.

I had been sick that week, so weak. Thank God I got her back. She has her Potty sheets so she does not go. We have found us a church we go to.

We love the people there. They are so nice just because I am writing about my life, I want people that read my book you have time to get ready before the rapture.

Ricky and I found us a Church we love so much. We have been going there for some time. We love the people. We feel at home there.

The people are real nice, the pastor Preacher Gods words. Beth, his wife is real nice to everyone. She loves the lord

I want people to know if you read my book. They have time to get ready.

Jesus is coming. I have books online about the rapture. Remember you may have a mother or a dad in heaven waiting on you, do not disappoint them.

I am so glad I turn my life around. I have a husband who goes to Church with me.

One day, I will see my family in heaven, don't you want to do that?

Repeat after, me dear Jesus I am a sinner please forgive me of all my sins 'come into my heart to live I will confess you to others. Amen

I need to go back when I was a little girl.

My grandma love me so much. If I was sick, she would hold me and pray for me.

When it was Saturday night, grandma would put rolls in my hair. The next morning she would comb it out for Church.

I would cry. She had a word for me, 'do not let the rats sleep in your hair', grandma no rats sleep in my hair.

I did not like it when she comb my hair, she pulled it out it would hurt.

That was my grandma. She was a sweet woman. She loved the lord.

I remember when she would eat, no teeth. She could eat like a beaver. Nothing was too hard for her.

I wonder how did she did it.

My grandma love to bake us cookies, cakes and anything she could cook on that old wood stove.

I love to watch her go to the garden, get fresh vegetables for us to eat.

When she was at our home, we never went hungry. She came there at the first of the month to get her check.

It was good to see her. She brought me something every time she came.

She did not put her money in a bank, she carried it on her.

The house I was born in, you could see it from the yard. I played with my brother Wallace and we played together. If we got into a fight, it was time out from one another.

We did not like that. I like picking blackberries. Mother would make us a pie.

When it snow, we had snow cream. Not anymore. The snow is bad now.

Walking to Church would hurt my feet. These things now are so much different than when I was growing up.

Instead of colored television, I saw a black and white one.

After School when my chores were done, then we went to the neighbor house. We watch western. It was ok for me I just wanted to go somewhere to play with other kids. We were told by mama before dark to come home.

We still played after we all watch television.

Remember one day I did not want to go to School? My sister stop by. She made a big thing out of me out of School. It made me mad, said something about it. She chases me down to the grapevine. I step on a piece of glass, wow that hurt. The blood was dripping everywhere in the house.

Mother pray for me. It put a sore on my foot after it quit bleeding. Mother was sorry I got hurt.

God was with us all the time. When it was stormy weather, it could get bad, we did not have lights.

We had lamp. That old house could stand anything. Just put some boards put together. You could her the wind outside, blowing it would last for a while. Just rain I could sleep like a Baby that old tin top, just rain.

Grandma made me pretty dresses not like hers. She had hers special made. I went with

Her one time to the house of the women made her nice dresses.

My grandma's clothes were most like long to her feet up to her neck. She never wore pants or shorts.

Any coffee and tea any television at my brothers they did have a little black and white

One. She asked them to turn it off when she undress.

I do not remember too much about grandma. I was a little girl not thinking of an older person except when I need something. Sorry to say that she spoils me. You know we may have been poor but we had the love that is something you cannot buy.

My mama love us and my Grandma, she was someone to fill in for Mama.

When she was sick, she stood in to take care of us.

Mama was in the field lots picking cotton. Grandma, I never saw her in the cotton fields. She may have brought mama water.

It was so bad in the fields. If you did not hurt your knees your hands would hurt

Mama, she would drag that old sack across the cotton patch so tired but she had to fill daddy shoes take care of us kids.

Paghat she went into the woods for firewood so we would have a warm room to get up in.

When we went to School, mama made the fire first thing in the morning. In Alabama it stay cold.

We live in the north part of the State where hills meet hill and carve meets carve. Where people pray for hours on their knees. Where Neighbors help each other. Where Churches everywhere.

The old county store mama would go to buy us grocers. I can see her coming down the road. Her dress swing in the wind.

Back then people thought about God morning, noon, and night. If people now had to do what we did back then.

I do not know how they would stand it.

God was with us many times. Our cow ate some poison, mama pray for her, we got milk the next day.

I met one of my friends at my mama's friends. We were all going to church. Her grandmother was the one she lived with close.

It was the first time I wore a pretty dress. She let me wear one of her dresses. I felt like a different person

My clothes were hand me downs and what mama and grandma made me out of flour sack.

We walked to the Church many times.

There were other people walked with us. Peggy and I sat on the same seat. We had to be quite.

Mama would get me when I got home if I was loud in Church.

The pastor of the church, he preach for a long time no watch we all went home when it was over.

Every time the Church was open we went mama never left us home unless when were sick, then someone stayed with us, God was with us. We never had to worry about someone coming to our School with a gun.

We prayed at night and Mama she was always praying lots on her knees.

She had a few friends that lived by us, Mrs. Fanny King and Mrs. Bevers.

There were some at church Mama Friends. I was a little girl

So I do not remember too much what happen. We lived on a mountain. you could see

Stevenson Alabama from our house.

We sometime would go down the mountain to the river. One thing I remember was a rock

That had a foot print on top of it. I was up there in 2011.

It was there when I was a little girl. After I left, I went back and could not find it.

I was thinking of take a picture of it. I do not know what happened to it

I was there in 2011 when the storms were bad. I found out something, after you leave you cannot go back, not the same Mama gone, my brothers are gone, the house is on the ground.

Just lots of memories left in that old house.

I found a little ball, I played with it. I was like a boy. All I had to play with was boys except when my kin came.

From Florida, there we play almost night. I miss my family. I know they are in heaven, see them.

I am so glad I came from a family that love the lord.

I remember one day when we thought a man had broken out of jail. They had it on the news.

We had to lock our doors. It was something we never had to worry about.

I went to spend the night with one of my friends from School. We had so much

Fun. Their family made candy. I was surprise mother let me go.

That was the only one time she let me go with. I did miss my family.

Never been away from home before. I got in trouble one time when I went with

My aunt sister to Tenn. my mother did not know where I was. I stay the night. I did not tell mother, I just left.

Mother was worried. Well, that is enough about me and my life the end.

The most important thing about my life is what happened to me when I was a toddler crawling around on the floor. I saw the kerosene can, I put it up and drink some of it. My brother Raymond saw what I had done. He call to mother attention. She pick me up and prayed for me. It has been so many years ago. Since then, Raymond was preaching. He told in his services that I was miracle Baby. Mother had faith God heal me because mother said I looked as white as a piece of cotton when she pick me up. You cannot out do God.

He is a healer. He is a provider. He is a miracle worker.

He is a Resurrection. He can the only way to heaven is though Jesus Christ my lord.

CPSIA information can be obtained
at www.ICGtesting.com
Printed in the USA
BVHW030241090320
574443BV00008B/5/J

9 781648 269936